# Dive In
# Face
# First!

It's
a
Wild
Life

Written and Illustrated by

## Michele Olzack

Ferne Press

Dive In Face First! It's a Wild Life

Copyright © 2012 by Michele Olzack

Illustrations by Michele Olzack
Illustrations created with pen and colored pencil
Layout and cover design by Susan Leonard

Printed in the United States.

Summary:
When a young heron leaves the nest in search of a new life, he encounters many creatures who make a tremendous impact on him.

Library of Congress Cataloging-in-Publication Data
Olzack, Michele
Dive In Face First! It's a Wild Life/Michele Olzack–First Edition
ISBN-13: 978-1938326-01-1
1. Self-help. 2. Fiction. 3. Courage. 4. Self-reliance. 5. Life journey.
I. Olzack, Michele II. Title
Library of Congress Control Number: 2012938170

FERNE PRESS

Ferne Press is an imprint of Nelson Publishing & Marketing
366 Welch Road, Northville, MI 48167
www.nelsonpublishingandmarketing.com
(248) 735-0418

For Harvey and Spike,
who will always
live long and prosper
in my heart.

# Acknowledgments

Thanks to my family, especially my mother, Nona, for the support, encouragement, and unfailing belief in my ability. You've made me realize the power of unconditional love. To my brother, Bill, your support was invaluable and your help understanding turtle behavior priceless.

Thanks to Jeff for introducing me to Harvey, supporting my efforts, and being a part of my journey.

Hugs to my ellipse doctor, mentor, and friend, Heiner Hertling, whose art inspires me. Thanks to my painting buddies, Ruth and Carl, for letting me join your paint group and motivating me with your skill and enthusiasm.

Special hugs to my graceful and stylish friend, Jean. Thanks for being my secret keeper. For my amazingly talented friend, Karen, I'm dazzled by your energy and many abilities.

Special thanks to my publisher, Marian Nelson, for prodding me to put my head in the water and allowing me to fulfill my writing and illustrating dreams. And thanks to Kris Yankee, my project manager and editor, for encouraging me to make a simple book into something more. Your steady hand has guided me through rough and uncertain water.

# Chapter One

K erplunk! Cough, cough. "HE—" cough "—LP!!"
The water burned his throat and eyes, and it
weighed down his feathers. He was struggling to take his
first breath. Water seeped in, covering his face and beak,
and threatened to sink him completely. He couldn't find
the strength to pull himself out of the blue half-shelled
egg that kept him underwater. It was over. His body
collapsed and he gave up!

"Hang on, Harvey! I'm here, Son!" a voice from far off,
almost in a tunnel, shouted at him.

He wanted to tell the voice to go away, that it was too
late. Then everything darkened. In the next instant, he
was flying upside down in the beak of a very large bird.
The wind rushed over his head, and he was dropped into
a pile of sticks and the waiting wings of yet another big
bird.

"Do you think he's okay?" Helen asked.

"He seems fine," Henry said as he patted the wet little
bird on the head. "No harm done."

But Harvey was far from fine. He was terrified! As he looked over the nest and into the murky pond, he knew that he never wanted to be face-first in water again. But he wouldn't think about that now. Instead, he blinked his eyes, getting rid of the water, and looked skyward. Above him were bare trees, gnarly limbs, and a group of large nests. In the nests were several prehistoric-looking birds feeding small downy balls of fluff. It was uncomfortably quiet and Harvey didn't like it.

"Where am I? Who am I?" he asked, confused and a little frightened.

"You're a great blue heron. You're going to be a majestic bird. We're your parents, and we live in a rookery. It's an island of large oak trees surrounded by shallow water. Our kind arrives every spring and builds colonies of nests that spread across the treetops like high-rise apartments. We work for days creating large platforms of sticks lined with pine needles and woven together with moss, reeds, and dry grasses. We're expert nest builders," his father explained with pride.

"Wow! Expert builders, huh?" Harvey looked around and noted the nest he was sitting in seemed to lack as many sticks as the others. In fact, it even had a few bare spots. "So what happened to ours? Seems like it's hanging in the wind."

"Dear, tell me again why we chose this spot?" Helen seemed puzzled as well.

"Because it was all that was left when we got here!" Henry snapped. "Remember, you wanted to spend extra time fishing in warm water. Then there was the detour you thought would help us catch the others, and it went downhill from there."

"Fine, so you're saying it's my fault."

---

**Helen and Henry, the Teenagers:**

One of the most difficult times in everyone's life is late adolescence. We take one step into adulthood and two steps back into the comfort zone of our childhood. We want to be treated as mature adults, but our actions are often self-centered. So we proceed without a clue through life. And we hope, like Harvey's parents, that we'll somehow produce a perfect heron.

---

"No, I didn't mean that. Let's not argue in front of Harvey. He's been through a terrible ordeal, and I bet he's hungry," his father suggested.

"Food would be good. What's for dinner?" Harvey asked excitedly.

"Just wait and I'll surprise you," his father said as he flew away over the treetops.

A few minutes later, he returned carrying a big fish. He dropped it next to Harvey and pulled pieces off with his large beak. Soon he was stuffing fish into Harvey's waiting mouth.

"Ooh, this is good," Harvey ate greedily. It was just right; firm and tangy, yet it easily slid down his throat. He loved it!

As the happy parents watched their son eat his first meal, a neighbor flew in and joined them.

"Just wanted to see how things were. I saw you took the brunt of the storm. That wind was really something. Did I see you stand up at one point?" the neighbor asked with concern.

"Yes, unfortunately my legs were getting cramped from sitting on the nest for so long. I guess I chose the worst moment. I didn't anticipate the wind would blow the nest apart," Helen replied.

"It was an exhausting process for us. I'm the one that encouraged her to stretch. But we never imagined this would happen," Henry admitted.

"Well, he's a cute little guy." The neighbor watched Harvey finish the last of the fish. "It's so sad the others didn't survive."

"What do you mean? There are no others," his father answered.

"You mean you only had one? That's amazing! We've got five," the neighbor said with a smirk. "Just as well, given the flimsy nest."

"Overachiever," Henry mumbled.

"Don't pay any attention to him," Helen said as she watched the other bird fly away. "Our Harvey is special and perfect in his own way."

"If I'm so perfect, why do I feel different?" Harvey mumbled, but before his parents could answer, he was sound asleep from his overstuffed belly.

The days passed quickly for Harvey. He had a voracious appetite for fish. His father looked exhausted from meeting his constant demands. One morning, Harvey sat on a dead limb that extended from the nest. His mother joined him as he marveled at all the changes in the rookery.

"I remember how scary this place was the first day I saw it."

"Yes, it's changed a lot," his mother admitted. "It's almost like magic."

The trees were lush, cattails wafted in the breeze, and beautiful wildflowers scented the air.

Harvey watched the Canada geese and swans circle the island with their new families, making introductions to the neighbors.

"What are those dark things in the water?" he asked.

"Muskrats," she explained. They watched in amusement as they darted in and out of the fallen logs along the shoreline.

Harvey laughed as he noticed several frogs hopping over the water lilies to lie in the sun on their iridescent pads. Meanwhile, multicolored butterflies darted among the wildflowers. The rookery was a whirl of activity. Herons circled throughout the day, bringing food to hungry offspring. While Harvey enjoyed the beauty and activity, he also sensed a change brought by a light breeze that rustled through the leaves. He became very quiet.

His mother snuggled closer to him and said, "The rookery isn't the only thing changing."

"What do you mean, Mom?" he asked while he looked around to see what he had missed.

"Well, you're not my ball of fluff anymore," Helen said sadly. "The down is almost gone and you've got beautiful, sleek blue-gray feathers. Your legs, which started as little yellow nubs, get longer every day. They're not fitting in the nest as easily anymore."

"I guess I'm growing," Harvey replied.

"You're a perfect blue heron." His mother smiled. "Look at you standing against the sky. Your neck has a classic S-shaped curve. You've got a long yellow beak designed for spearing fish."

"It's time to learn to fly and catch your own fish," his father told him as he joined them on the limb.

"What a fine idea," his mother said.

The flying part was easy. As his father balanced him on the nest, he stretched his wings and soared into the sky. The air rushed against his face and ruffled his feathers. He was amazed at how high he soared and how weightless he felt.

"It's so quiet up here, yet I can hear fish jumping in the water," Harvey said to his father, who flew next to him. "I want to swoop down. Wheee!" He felt his stomach flip-flop as he dove downward. Just as quickly, he soared up. He was hooked on flying, and he flipped and dove repeatedly. Mostly, he liked the control of his body. He could get close enough to smell the pond water, but by pulling upward, he never got his head wet!

The fishing was another issue. No matter how many times his father demonstrated the swoop and landing in the water, Harvey couldn't do it.

"If you can't land in the water, just walk into it," Henry pleaded. "Then you can put your head in the water and grab some minnows."

Harvey would land on a rock or on the grass and walk on skinny stilt legs to the edge and look sadly into the water.

"No way!" Harvey cried. "I'm not sticking my head in that water."

He would shake his head no. Then he would fly back to the nest and his mother. Harvey knew his father would eventually give up and bring him a fish, and that made him happy.

*When we're trying to overcome our fears or unable to meet our basic needs, it's hard to believe in our own unique talents.*

The other little herons made fun of him. They watched him walk carefully to the edge of the water but never get wet.

"Look at Harvey! He's afraid of water. He's hopeless—he'll never learn to fish."

The ridicule never ended until Harvey flew away. They made him feel sad by what they said. But he refused to feel hopeless.

One night, when his parents thought he was asleep in the nest, he overheard them talking.

*Try to drown out the dissenting voices in your life. Learn to listen and respect your inner voice because it already knows where to lead you.*

"What are we going to do about Harvey?" his father complained. "I can't feed him fish forever. He's got to learn to take care of himself."

"It's our fault Harvey's different," his mother sadly admitted. "But our boy is special in his own way. We just have to take care of him."

8

Harvey felt tears in his eyes as he listened to his parents talk. He didn't want to be a burden. He decided to take action.

The next morning just before sunrise, when his mother was sleeping and his father was off catching the first fish, Harvey flew out of the nest. He didn't know where to go, but he didn't want his parents finding him. He was determined that eventually they would be proud of him.

"Bye, Mom and Dad. I love you," he said as he glanced back.

With butterflies in his stomach, he flew toward his future.

When we start the journey to find our life's quest, we hope the GPS will guide us down the quickest road with the smoothest pavement. In reality, we often misinterpret the signal and find more roadblocks, detours, and potholes than we ever expected.

# Chapter Two

Harvey soared through the treetops, along the riverbanks, and across meadows strewn with beautiful wildflowers. As he flew, he felt tired but confident he was far from his nest. Finally, Harvey landed on a grassy area along a bend in the river. The cattails rustled in the breeze and an old willow let its bent limbs drift lazily in the water. He walked carefully to the edge, peered down into the clear water, and shook his head.

---

### Harvey, the Seeker:

We search for so many things in life—love, belonging, a sense of self-worth, the strength to overcome our fears, and sometimes just the elusive happiness. As we struggle to find what we need in life, we forget to embrace the journey. Try to start each day as a new beginning and imagine the possibilities.

---

"Now what do I do? I'm tired and hungry, but I'm not putting my head in that river," he announced.

"So how are you going to eat?" a little voice behind him asked.

Harvey turned and saw a squirrel sitting next to him. "I don't know. Got any suggestions?"

"How about a nut?" the little squirrel asked and tossed him a plump acorn.

Harvey was hungry enough to eat anything, so he grabbed it with his beak and swallowed it whole. "Not very flavorful and a little hard and lumpy going down."

"You're supposed to crack it before you eat it. Watch me!" The squirrel grabbed another acorn, cracked it with his big teeth, and ate the inside. "Mmm, tasty!"

"The problem is I don't have teeth." Harvey sighed. "This is not going to work. Do you have anything smaller?"

"Maybe you'd enjoy some sunflower seeds. Lots of birds like those, plus you can break them open with your long beak."

"That's the ticket!" Harvey fanned his wings with excitement. "Where do I get them?"

"Best place is a sunflower." The squirrel scratched his head. "It'll be a month before they bloom though."

"So what do I do till then? Eat roadkill?" Harvey grimaced with disgust.

"You really are pathetic." The squirrel shook his head. "Follow me. I'll show you a secret place and introduce you to some friends of mine. Maybe they can help you."

The squirrel turned and headed quickly toward the brush. Meanwhile, Harvey struggled to keep up the squirrel's pace. He walked slowly, carefully avoiding limbs and thorns that might destroy his perfect feathers. Occasionally, the squirrel looked back and waved impatiently.

### Squirrel, the Passerby:

There are people I call passersby in life. We often mistakenly call them friends. They seem helpful, but they're not really invested in our well-being. They're too quick to push us off on someone else or get rid of us if we don't serve their purpose. Choose your friends wisely! Otherwise, you'll be inundated with those who pass through and just as quickly say goodbye.

"Can't you hurry up? I thought you were hungry."

"Ouch! I just stubbed my foot on a rock," Harvey whined. "Yeah, I'm hungry. But birds fly, remember?"

"Just get a move on it. We'll miss the best seeds."

The squirrel turned and ran even faster. He leaped over small rocks and logs, while Harvey struggled to catch up. Just as Harvey had given up hope of reaching the secret destination, he saw the squirrel sitting on a large rock behind some tall grasses.

"Okay, so where are we? Better still, where's the seed?" He panted with exhaustion.

"Take a look." The squirrel parted some of the grasses with his paw. Harvey stretched his long neck through the remaining weeds and looked out. There was a large stretch of groomed lawn with an asphalt sidewalk stretching down toward a glassed building.

"Pretty path, but I'm not getting it yet." Harvey was becoming more and more frustrated.

"Bird brain, this is the single best seed spot in the park! The chipmunks, squirrels, and small birds get fed here year round," the squirrel explained while tapping his foot impatiently.

"You mean the seed is stored in that place and everybody helps themselves?" Harvey exclaimed. He thought there might be hope for a meal after all.

"Are you stupid?" The squirrel cocked his head to the side. "I'm only telling you once. Try to keep up. The building is a nature center. For some unknown reason, humans love the place. On the way out, they carry seed. They drop it on the pathway. It's a gold mine for chipmunks, squirrels, and little birds. We get to eat, and they have a photo op. It's a win-win deal!"

"Cool! So how do I get some action?" Harvey flapped his wings with excitement.

"Let me see what I can do." As he parted the tall grass, the squirrel looked up and down the walkway. "Look, there's a chipmunk stuffing his cheeks. Hey, Charlie! Can you join me on the rock for a minute?"

The chipmunk ran to the rock and jumped up next to the squirrel. His cheeks were so full, it seemed impossible for him to hold another seed.

"Can you share some birdseed with my friend? He's starving!"

Charlie looked puzzled as he considered
Harvey. Then, shrugging his shoulders,
he spit all the food in his cheeks out
onto the rock. He gave Harvey
a large toothy grin, turned,
and ran back to
the walkway.

"Recycled bird seed—yum!" Harvey cringed.

"Beggars can't be choosers!" The squirrel put his
hands on his hips and glared. "You should be thankful for
Charlie's generosity. He probably worked all afternoon to
get that seed."

"Can I help it if I don't like leftovers? But I see your
point. I am ungrateful. Maybe I could pick up seed myself
and not bother the others," he offered.

"Oh boy, I don't know. That's a sticky issue. Let me
think." The squirrel put his paw on his head and was quiet
for a moment. "I don't know if it will work, but I do know

we'll need a conference." The squirrel jumped off the rock and ran down the path. He signaled Harvey to stay put. As he ran he called out, and soon three chipmunks joined him. Harvey watched them get into a huddle on the pathway. From the way the chipmunks chattered and gestured, it seemed like an animated conversation. Periodically the littlest chipmunk glared in Harvey's direction. Finally the conference broke and the squirrel returned to the rock, leaving the three chipmunks on the pathway.

"There are a lot of issues to consider," the squirrel said with a serious tone. "First of all, Cindy thinks you're vertically challenged. She thinks you'll frighten the humans. Second, Charlie thinks you won't respect boundaries. They work from the park bench to the fence and they want you to stay away from that area. Finally, this might be the most concerning problem. The little guy, Peanut, thinks you're eyeing him. He thinks you're sizing him up as a dinner choice. Got any answers?"

Harvey shook his head and let out a deep breath. "Okay, so I'm tall. But I can be cute. Next, I know how to respect someone's territory. After all, I'm a heron. I was raised in a rookery where all the nests look alike. Except my family's, but that's another story. We never mistakenly fly into the wrong nest. But as for Peanut's remarks, that's possible. Herons do eat small rodents along with fish."

As he said this, all three chipmunks sat up, threw their paws in the air, and shrieked.

"Joking guys, I never eat rodent. When the fishing was bad, my father brought a mouse. I had indigestion for a week," Harvey reassured them. "Besides, there have been reports of herons suffocating while eating too large a rodent. So, no worries with me."

The squirrel and chipmunks looked at each other and nodded. "We'll let you give it a try, but nobody is hopeful."

As directed, Harvey stayed behind the rock. Before long, a mother and her small son came out of the nature center door. As promised, the boy carried a sack of seed.

"Look Mom, there are chipmunks everywhere." The boy jumped up and down with excitement. "Should I start passing out the seed?"

"Sure, let's start with the little guy in front of you. He's sitting up so cute. Drop him some seed and I'll get a picture." She quickly pulled out her camera, just as the boy cautiously let Peanut eat out of his hand. "Wait until Grandma sees this one!"

They continued to move along, feeding the other two chipmunks and the squirrel. A chickadee landed on the boy's hand, and he squealed with excitement.

"Nothing to it!" Harvey exclaimed as he watched them move closer. As they moved up the pathway, he stepped out from behind the rock. He assumed his friendliest pose and waited his turn.

## Chipmunks, the Dependents:

Dependency is the inability to live without support from others. At its best, it makes life easy. But when we're dependent, what do we learn by taking the easy way out? We become increasingly helpless waiting for a handout from a generous person. What happens to people who are dependent during the un-expected storm?

At first the boy was too busy looking down to notice him. Suddenly, he reached Harvey's feet and looked up his long body. When they were eye to eye, when he gave a loud scream. "Mom! What is it?"

"Um—I think a blue heron! I've never seen one this close," she replied.

"What do I do? It's staring at me!"

"Oh, just drop the seed already. How hard can it be?" Harvey grimaced with frustration.

"Mom, I don't like it!" the little boy cried.

"Give it some seed, and let's get out of here," she replied.

The boy threw down the seed. Then, the mother grabbed her son's hand and they ran up the walkway.

"That went well," the squirrel said sarcastically as he watched Harvey scarf seed.

"Crazy kid, afraid of a heron." Harvey broke open several shells with his beak.

"Looks who's talking, Mister I-can't-put-my-head-in-the-water-like-a-normal-heron," the squirrel admonished him.

"Okay, it didn't go like I expected. Besides, I'd need buckets of this stuff to feel full. Any other suggestions?" Harvey inquired hopefully.

When we take the easy way out or settle for any happy meal, is our life's hunger really satisfied? Or is it just a bunch of empty calories?

"Time to go, Harvey. I've helped all I can." The squirrel shook his head sadly. "I think you're hopeless."

"Don't use that word. I hate that. But you were right; this is the land of the little creatures. I don't belong." He put his head down and sighed.

"It's a big park, Harvey. You'll find your place," the squirrel said encouragingly.

"Thanks for your time. Say goodbye to the others. They were great."

We only believe we are hopeless and pathetic when we allow others to define us.

With a quick look back, he lifted his wings, leaped into the air, and headed skyward.

# Chapter Three

Flying never failed him. He was exhilarated by the wind rushing against his face, yet calmed by the stillness, broken only by the beating of his wings against the air. There was only one problem with flying—eventually he had to land. As Harvey circled around the sky, he didn't have a clue where to go next. He was more exhausted than hungry. As the sun dipped lower, he chose a large oak tree to rest for the night. The tree reminded him of home; comforted, he slept soundly. He dreamed of easily catching fish. In the morning, he woke to a growling stomach. As he flew from the tree to the ground, he realized the tree was isolated in a large field with grass and wildflowers.

"Well, I won't find any fish here. Despite what I said to the others yesterday, I think I'm hungry enough to eat a dozen field mice."

He looked around as he talked to himself and contemplated where to look for a mouse.

"On second thought, they go down with a thud, not to mention they have a wild, earthy taste. Yuck! Maybe

I should fly back to the river." He was annoyed. "Right, like the fish are going to jump out of the water and into my mouth."

"It's possible," a little voice answered. "Haven't you ever heard of flying fish?"

Harvey looked down, and a small rabbit was pulling on clover and chewing as he talked. The rabbit made the clover look so tempting, Harvey's mouth watered.

"Mind if I join you?" he asked. "I'm awfully hungry."

"There's plenty to eat here. Help yourself," the rabbit answered. "Look at all the delicious options." The rabbit sat up and pointed at the grasses, flowers, and twigs.

"They're crunchy. Lots of fiber," Harvey commented as he chewed on a small stick. "But they're hard to swallow and not much flavor."

"Then try some grass and quit complaining," the rabbit said as he happily munched on some weeds.

"Yuck, it's bland." Harvey gagged as he struggled with a mouthful of grass. "What are you? Some sort of herbivore?"

"No, I'm Spike. Not Herby." The rabbit looked up, and then continued stuffing his mouth with weeds.

"What I mean is, are you a plant eater?"

"Yep, that's me. I'm all about roots and shoots."

"So far, I'm not impressed with the shoots. Are the roots any better?" Harvey inquired with as much optimism as he could muster.

"If you hop along with me, I'll show you some of the sweetest carrots to die for," Spike beckoned.

"Let's be clear. I'm a heron and we don't hop. When we walk, we glide slowly and gracefully," Harvey said proudly and preened his feathers while he talked.

"Okay, Your Grace. Why don't you glide slowly, while I take you to my special carrot spot?" Spike looked over his shoulder and took off hopping.

"The things I put up with for some lousy food," Harvey grumbled.

As he said it, he realized Spike was vanishing and that he'd never keep up. So he took to the air and was able to follow the bouncing cottontail that easily leaped through the grasses. A short time later, he found himself at the edge of a large garden. Spike was busily uprooting large carrots. He tossed them on the grass and awaited Harvey's arrival.

"Look at these beauties," Spike proclaimed as he proudly dangled a carrot from his paws. "Dig in and enjoy! These are the sweetest things you've ever tasted."

"They smell fresh, but I have no teeth to eat them," Harvey moaned.

"That is a problem. Why don't you try some greens instead? They're just as flavorful." As he said it, he bit off the greens from several carrots and tossed them to Harvey.

"They're delicious—tender and sweet," Harvey admitted and proceeded to consume all the greens Spike offered. "I must be starving because I usually only eat fish."

"Then why aren't you fishing instead of standing around and taking up my airspace?" Spike asked with irritation, but continued chewing his carrot.

"I've got this little issue with water," Harvey quietly admitted and put his head down. "I can't put my head or feet in it."

"Afraid you'll drown, huh?" Spike laughed.

"Well, I'm not like you," Harvey said defensively. "You've got this carefree existence. You've got a beautiful meadow, and you're able to enjoy your favorite foods."

"So, you think it's always been that way and I've never had to struggle, right? Let me tell you a story." Spike stopped chewing and tilted his head. "I wasn't born in this field. I used to be a family pet. They called me Hopper."

"That's not a bad name," Harvey interrupted.

"Kind of generic. It's like calling you Fisher," Spike replied.

"I wouldn't mind if it were true." Harvey lowered his eyes. "But the name's Harvey."

"Well how 'bout calling you hopeless," he said with annoyance.

"Now you're getting personal. I get it. Just finish the story."

"At first, the family who owned me really seemed to care. I got brushed all the time and played with. But that didn't last long because they got a puppy. They put me in a box and left me in the basement where it was dark, damp, and cold. Sometimes they even forgot to feed me. The little girl who had spent time with me never bothered anymore. I was really sad. One day there was a storm and the basement flooded."

"Why does fear always start with water?" Harvey shuddered.

"At least it got me out of the basement and back behind their garage," Spike continued. "But they didn't bother with me at all out there. As time passed, I knew I had to get out. It took me forever and I lost a tooth in the process, but I finally got the door open and I took off. I never looked back. I changed my name to Spike because it seemed adventurous."

"Weren't you afraid?

"Sure I was. I didn't know where to find food or what to do. Unlike you, I couldn't fly. Trust me, there are lots of things out there that want to eat rabbits, like coyotes, foxes, cats, and even dogs."

"It sounds horrible. How did you survive?" Harvey asked with new appreciation for his friend.

"It wasn't easy. I found a few wild rabbits to give me guidance. Then I got lucky and found this place."

### Spike, the Visionary:

It's easy to believe some people are born with the proverbial silver spoon in their mouth. We think they've always been wealthy, gifted, or highly successful. We certainly can't be like them because we weren't born with the same advantages. So we couldn't possibly be held to the same achievement level. But, if we look closely at some of the incredible people we admire, we might see something else. Many come from humble or disadvantaged backgrounds. But they possess the strength, the courage, and the determination to be something more. They seem to have an inner vision that lights their way. Or perhaps they just have the intelligence to realize that in their darkest moments they have nothing left to lose by moving forward. Maybe we should follow!

"What do you see when you look in front of you?" Spike stood on his hind legs and made a sweeping gesture with his paw.

"I see some grass and pretty flowers. That's about it," Harvey admitted.

"Well, I see a rainbow. Just over that rise is a beautiful red barn, and they have the freshest hay I've ever eaten. They have a bunch of apple trees with the sweetest fruit you've ever tasted. In late summer, there are blueberry and raspberry bushes. I eat so much that the juice runs down my cheeks and mats my fur. Those flowers in the field smell so fragrant and taste so good. And these carrots are the crunchiest. There are melons, squash, and vegetables to enjoy. I could go on and on. This is the best place on Earth. It's worth all the trouble it took to find it."

"I wish I could find that kind of place." Harvey shut his eyes and imagined.

"It's out there waiting for you. Just not in my field. It's not that you're not welcome. You just will never belong here," Spike told him.

"You're right." Harvey said. "But I don't have a clue where to look next."

"I think in our darkest moments, when we're the most lost, that's when we find ourselves. Maybe we simply have nothing left to lose," he stated.

*Without action, a vision is just another crazy dream.*

Then, looking directly at Harvey, Spike added, "So, off you go. Find your rainbow, Harvey!"

# Chapter Four

Harvey soared as high as possible in an attempt to touch the clouds. He was giddy with thoughts of rolling carefree in the fluffy marshmallow sky. Spike had inspired him, and he felt confident he would find his personal rainbow.

But where should he look next? The thought troubled him as he glided effortlessly through the air. Suddenly he hit turbulence in an updraft and it was like slamming into a brick wall. That's when he saw the river. The answer was obvious; his rainbow would always be at the water, the place he feared yet needed the most. He swooped down and landed in a grassy spot adjacent to a gently flowing stream. It was time to confront the demons.

We have moments of clarity when we quiet the chaos in our lives. If we allow ourselves to take that time, the world falls away and we're left with a magical sense of purpose.

"I can do this. I can do this!" he chanted as he walked back and forth. "No, I can't! No, I can't!" The argument with himself continued until he looked toward the river. A beautiful swan floated by with her five little ones trailing behind her. Harvey walked to the edge of the water and called to her.

"Could you please help me? I'm very hungry, but I'm a little afraid to get in the water," he sadly admitted.

"Don't be afraid. It's shallow near the edge," Mother Swan encouraged. "You've got long legs. You can walk right in."

Harvey took his leg and slowly tried to step in. But the minute he felt wet, he pulled back and shivered. "I can't do it. How did you teach your kids to swim?"

"They just naturally love the water," Mother Swan said affectionately. "Plus, it helps to have webbed feet. But you have a long neck. Maybe you could just dip it in the shallow water and catch some minnows."

"Uh—no!" He shook his head. "It's the water thing. I just can't do it."

"Mama, is there something wrong with that bird?" one of the little swans asked, as the other four laughed at Harvey's predicament. "He seems a little crazy. The other herons we've talked to don't have that issue."

"Quiet, children!" Mother Swan scolded. "It's not nice to laugh or make fun of someone just because they're different."

## Mother Swan and the Cygnets,
## the Wise Grandma and the Naysayers:

There are people in our lives who are quick to criticize and ridicule us. They may be too young to know better or older and set in their ways. It doesn't matter what we do, we don't conform to their idea of normal. We'll always be a square peg trying to fit into a round hole. When we encounter those people, it helps if we have the support of a wise grandma, mother, or friend. They take pride in our uniqueness and offer us sound advice. Most important, they provide us with unconditional love and a sense of direction.

DIVE IN FACE FIRST! IT'S A WILD LIFE

Harvey hung his head and sat down on a flat rock by the stream. He was hungry and not in the mood to be laughed at. Besides, reality was causing his earlier optimism to fade.

"Don't feel sad," Mother Swan said. "We'll think of something to help you. Oh, look. Here come Gus and Gracie. Maybe they can help."

Harvey looked up and saw two large Canada geese gliding gracefully through the water.

"What's happening, Mama? Did you put something in the weeds? Those kids get bigger every time I see them," one of them said as they floated to the swans.

"They are something, aren't they?" Mother Swan beamed. "Gus, can you help me with a problem? My friend has an issue with fishing. He's really hungry, and I don't know how to help."

"I don't know. Can you think of anything, Gracie?"

"Didn't we just pass a fishing pier?" Gracie asked. "You were complaining about the humans catching fish and tossing them back in. You said that's why there's sometimes dead fish floating on the water."

"That's right! Let's go back and see if they left any today." Both geese turned and headed upstream.

"Oh, good. They'll help you." Mother Swan told Harvey. "Children! What did I tell you about staying together? Do you want the garpike to eat you? I'm sorry, I have to catch them. I know some bad children who will be sitting on shore the rest of the day." She swam off with her wings angrily fluffed. Her children were headed downstream, laughing hysterically as the current spun them in circles.

Harvey yelled a quick "thank you" to Mother Swan and then paced back and forth with mounting impatience. It felt strange, like he was back in the nest waiting for his father to return with the morning fish. But he quickly overcame the feeling as he spotted Gus and Gracie floating back. They each carried a fish in their strong beaks.

"Sweet!" Harvey yelled as they stepped up on the shore and dropped the fish at his feet. "You guys saved me!"

He ate both fish whole. They slid down with that pungent delectable flavor he had almost forgotten. With a satisfied sigh, he sat down on the grass. His stomach was finally full and it was time for a nap.

"You know those fish were dead. Eventually, they drift onto shore. I can tell you exactly where to find them," Gus offered.

"You guys did a great job. I can't thank you enough," Harvey said as he opened one sleepy eye. "I'll be here tomorrow waiting for you."

Gracie studied Gus. "I think we may have a problem on our hands."

"Yep," Gus agreed. Both geese swam off shaking their heads.

True to his word, Harvey was there the next day and the next few days after that. Each day the geese floated in with an offering of fish. Harvey was feeling brave enough to sit on a big rock in the middle of the stream. By doing so, he could see them coming and then leap to the shore and wait for his meal. He always insisted they bring the fish to him. He might sit on rocks, but he was not about to let his feet touch the water. He was happy he had come back to the river.

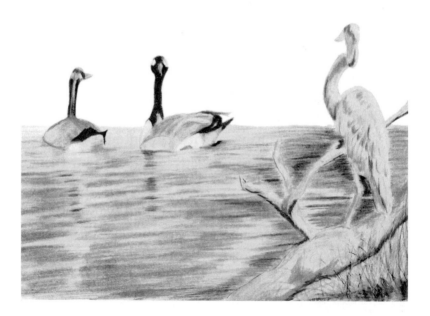

## Gus and Gracie, the Enablers:

An enabler is someone who through his or her actions allows someone else to achieve something. The enabler may act out of love, the need to please, and/or misguided helpfulness in an attempt to protect a person. But he or she is actually making the problem worse. This leads to a vicious cycle of codependency, where neither party is able to move forward and grow. Breaking the cycle is enormously difficult. It requires distinguishing needed help from imposed harm. Often it takes strength of will and an ability on the part of the enabler to feel comfortable with the word no.

One morning after a full meal, he announced to the geese, "This is the best! I may have found my rainbow!"

"I found my rainbow! Woohoo!" a voice mocked him from above. "More like a thundercloud sitting over your fool head."

Harvey squinted his eyes and looked up. Sitting on a limb above him was the largest bald eagle he had ever seen. His white head gleamed in the sunlight. His body was large and powerful, thickly covered with feathers. He had huge talons, sharpened to fine points. He was an intimidating sight, and both geese shuddered convulsively.

"I've been watching you." He glared at Harvey. "Only a lazy sissy bird lets a couple of ducks feed him. So you can't put your head in the water. Boohoo!"

"Excuse me, Mr. Eagle, sir. Gracie and I are not ducks," Gus interjected and then proudly added, "We're Canada geese."

"Well, do you have webbed feet?"

"Uh, actually we do," Gus admitted.

"Then, you're ducks, right?" the eagle persisted.

"To be accurate, we have graceful long necks and large bodies. Ducks are actually much smaller and their necks are short," Gus lectured, while Gracie nodded her head in agreement.

The eagle stepped out on the farthest tip of the branch and leveled both geese with a penetrating stare. "If I say you're ducks, then you're ducks! I'm tired of this discussion. Now, quack on out of here before I scratch your eyes out with my razor-sharp talons."

"Right, then. We're so a couple of ducks. Quack! Quack! C'mon Gracie, let's quack on out of here." Gus turned abruptly and paddled upstream with Gracie quacking all the way behind him.

"Now that's what I call fun!" The eagle let out a menacing laugh.

"You're not a very nice guy." Harvey gave him a look of disdain.

"Let me give you your first lesson in life; there's no future in being nice."

"There's no future in being a bully, either. You shouldn't be that way," Harvey persisted.

"I'm the biggest, the brightest, and the best. I can be whatever I want," the eagle proudly exclaimed.

Choose to stand up for the people who can't stand up for themselves-not because it makes you a hero but because it's the right thing to do.

"Whatever you say, B-Cubed. What do you want from me?" Harvey asked skeptically.

"Get up on this branch and we'll discuss it." The eagle motioned with his shiny white head.

Harvey flew up onto the limb and bravely sat close to the eagle.

"Be careful of my tail feathers! I worked all morning to preen them. I just got them to lie perfectly straight," he complained. "Ouch. I think you stepped on my claw and busted a talon!"

"You told me to fly up on the branch. Can I help it if it's a tight squeeze?"

"Sit on the inner portion of the limb and give me some personal space. I want anyone that passes by to notice my perfection."

### B-Cubed, the Legend in His Own Mind:

We've either met this person or been exposed to him through popular media. He's the epitome of success and seeks to constantly remind us of that fact. He may bully, belittle, or bedazzle those around him. He seems to want others to believe the impressive persona he has created. Don't you wonder what image he sees when he looks in the mirror each morning?

Harvey shook his head but moved away and no longer crowded the eagle.

"That's better." He sighed deeply. "Now we can discuss your situation. From what I've observed, you're a pathetic case. You and I are from the same food chain, but of course I'm higher up. We're predators and competitors. We should be fighting for the same fish. Of course, I'd be the one to win."

Harvey interrupted before the eagle could continue. "About the fish thing. Have you considered fishing for humility lately?"

"And have you considered that I can poke your eyes out with my talons? It doesn't apply just to ducks." He glared at Harvey.

"Water, I'm afraid of. You, not so much," Harvey said without a blink as the eagle took a menacing step toward him.

"I'll give you credit; you're kind of plucky," the eagle replied.

"I don't know about that. I still can't put my head in the water, and you got rid of my floating meal delivery," Harvey said sadly.

"Something tells me you'll work it out. You're a lot stronger than you think. I have confidence in you, and that's saying something. I seldom believe in anyone but me." The eagle winked at him.

"I'm glad someone believes in me. I'm still not so sure about myself."

"Harvey, it's a new day filled with opportunity. Think of the possibilities."

The eagle spread his wings and soared into the air. Looking back at Harvey, he added, "See you on the water, kid!"

# Chapter Five

Harvey flew onto a large log at the edge of the shore. He was trying hard to find the strength and courage.

"If B-Cubed thinks I have it, then it must be there," he said to himself as he gazed into the water. The image that reflected back was of a strong, handsome heron that should be capable of great things. He looked deeper into the water and saw several minnows float by. They seemed so near the surface.

"I'll bet if I just put my beak in there, I could grab one. I wouldn't have to put my head in. I don't think I can drown if I just put my beak in." To prove the point to himself, he lowered his head until his beak almost touched the top of the water.

Immediately, his head shot up. "Ohhh, I'm going to be sick. I can't do it! No way!"

We are limited only by our self-doubt.

"What's your problem, dude?"

Harvey turned his head and saw four turtles sitting on the log.

"I'm hungry, dizzy, and very tired. I want fish. I can't figure out how to get them, and I don't know what else to eat."

"If you'd stop blocking our sunlight, maybe we could help you." The largest turtle glared at Harvey.

"I don't know. I'm kind of discouraged. What do you guys eat?"

"Just about anything. We dive down, grab something that looks good, and eat it quickly."

"The eating quick part I could get into. But it's a definite NO to the diving."

"You're not like a turtle," the littlest guy piped up. "We never get discouraged, and we're very persistent. You might even say we're downright stubborn."

### Turtles, the Stubborn Optimists:

Is the food better or the grass really greener on the other side? We need to be careful that our stubborn persistence isn't really irrational impulse. Gather your facts and think carefully before moving blindly into a new situation, or the light at the end of the tunnel might turn out to be an oncoming train.

"That's true," another one added. "No matter the obstacle, we never give up. My brother was a good example of that. There's a road that goes across a waterway. We were on one side and the food was good, but my brother thought it would be better on the opposite side."

He moved closer to the other turtles
as he talked. "It would have taken
time, but we could have swum
around it. Instead, my
brother insisted on
crossing the road.

We walk slowly, so that was difficult as well. It was
also very scary. Humans in big machines were dodging
us and making noise. At one point, I almost got run over.
But in the end, we made it. And he was right; the food
was better and fresher on that side."

"So the moral of the story is this," the last one
interjected. "When you want to overcome an obstacle
in life, you must be determined, persistent, and a little
stubborn like a turtle."

"Actually I think I'm hearing a different moral to
that story," Harvey interjected. "I think if you don't
acknowledge the fears in life, and you act impulsively,
you could get squashed."

"You're hopeless, dude. Sorry. We've tried, but we
can't help you," the largest turtle responded. "Now get
going before we lose our sunlight."

"I'm not hopeless! Can't a guy have a different point of view? I'm frustrated and hungry, but not hopeless!" Harvey shot back. Then he flapped his wings and headed into the sky.

He landed on a pylon and faced a marina of boats rocking happily in the breeze. The sun was warm on his face, and he closed his eyes and imagined he

*If you believe you are not hopeless, you won't be.*

could plunge into the warm water below and catch the biggest fish that swam by. It was a comforting thought, and he basked in the glow. An unexpected nudge at his side caused him to open his eyes and look down beside him. A seagull perched next to him as though it was the most natural thing for two different birds to do.

"Sorry, but you're on my pylon. Fortunately, I don't mind sharing," the gull announced agreeably.

"Oh, I didn't know the pylons were labeled," Harvey answered honestly. He looked sideways and saw there were several empty ones available. "Looks like there's plenty to go around."

"This is the best one for me to keep track of the grass, sidewalks, and parking lot for my team. I'm on lookout duty today."

Harvey ignored the comment because it didn't make sense. He preferred to look skyward. As he did, he noticed several other gulls performing amazing stunts.

They looped, flipped, and dove sideways through the air. One bird hovered above him and he seemed so still it was like he floated on air.

"How do you guys do that?" he asked with envy.

"We're born acrobats. We're skilled at making impossible antics look effortless."

"That's so cool! It must be wonderful to be so carefree."

"We're not carefree. We have important work to do, and we take our job seriously," the gull stated.

"Still, I'd like to have your skills. I'd spend my day free-falling through the air, and I'd have constant fun and laughs. At least you don't have a water phobia like me."

"Are you serious? No one spends his day just having fun, especially a seagull. The key to life is finding balance. We all have a purpose and something we're supposed to do. If we have fun while we're doing it, then that's the best we can hope for." The seagull lectured Harvey like he was a small child.

Most of us only see what we don't have. We're so jealous of others, we can't see beyond our noses or beaks.

"Okay, so it's not all laughs, but where's the bad?" He remained unconvinced.

"Well, the humans consider us a nuisance. Since we come together in groups, they're always screaming and chasing us away. They don't understand what we're about."

The seagull looked back and forth, scanning the grassy area as he talked. "We actually perform a valuable service for them. Humans are not very clean, and they are not careful with their large machines. When they leave an area, there's trash everywhere. Also, they go very fast and often run over small animals. We scavenge up all the dead animals and organic litter. If no one took care of that waste, it would become toxic and threaten humans and all of us. We have an incredible digestive system and we're happy to do our part. It would just be nice if we sometimes got a little gratitude for our hard work."

"Wow, I never knew that. But let me be the first to say thanks for all you do," Harvey said with admiration for his new friend.

"Gee, thanks. This is the first time anyone ever thanked me," the gull responded.

"Ahh, isn't that sweet. You two are so special," a mocking voice said from above.

Harvey looked up and saw B-Cubed perched on a tall flagpole. He had to admit that the eagle was a magnificent-looking bird backlit by a cloudless blue sky.

"Why do I get the impression you're following me?"

"I am watching you, but today is all about me. Once a week I perch on this pole after I'm nice and full of tender, juicy fish," he tormented Harvey. "For some reason, the humans love to see me here. They gather to watch and take photos of me. It's like I'm some kind of icon. So when I have time, I come here to give my fans a thrill and let them pay homage to my magnificence."

"Oh, boy, is that guy full of himself or what?" the gull whispered.

"Ya think? He's got quite the overactive ego," Harvey replied just as quietly.

"I hear you! An eagle has superb vision and even better hearing, and you two are starting to annoy me." B-Cubed squinted his eyes at both birds, but turned to Harvey and said, "It occurs to me that you can't soar with the eagle if you sit with the seagulls."

"I have no problem sitting with seagulls. They do important work. You couldn't be at the top, like you think you are, if they weren't down below cleaning up after you," Harvey shot back.

## Seagulls, the Invisible Workers:

They clean our offices while we sleep, sweep the floors long after we've left the building, and pick up the trash while most of us are at work. We pass them by without acknowledgment and seldom give them a second thought, unless, of course, we find something amiss. If the waste can is full or the bathroom unclean, blame housekeeping. If we come home to trash left on the grass, it must be the lousy garbage collector. We never notice them until something we take for granted is not done. We forget they're the foundation of every successful organization or clean yard. The next time you pass an invisible worker, give them a smile or a wave. Better still, take a moment to thank them for all they do.

"Those gulls are nothing more than lowlife garbage collectors," he retorted.

"The politically correct term is sanitation engineers. And don't ever call us lowlifes again!" the gull screamed and flew toward the eagle. The other gulls followed in close pursuit. Soon there were several circling him.

"I don't need to be politically correct," he said arrogantly. "But I'll tell you one thing; there's a no-fly zone around an eagle. Now get out of here, you pesky scavengers."

"We'll leave when you show us respect!" one shouted as the others continued to circle.

"I'll show you respect. I have a real appreciation for each of you as a dinner choice. I'll break the first scrawny neck that touches me and pick your bones clean. Now that's something I could really value." B-Cubed smirked.

"Let's get out of here, guys, before we lose a team member." The gulls circled one last time and headed as a flock toward the beach. The gull that had been sitting with Harvey nodded his head goodbye and took off after the others.

> Those behind the scenes are an integral part of the whole, and we need to appreciate them.

"You totally need to get over yourself, dude." Harvey shook his head.

"I'll get over myself about as soon as you buck up and put your head in the water. I'm guessing that won't be anytime soon." He laughed. "Now get out of here before you distract my human admirers. And don't forget, I'll see you on the water, kid."

# Chapter Six

Harvey landed on a rocky shoreline. Sea grasses and moss covered the rocks, and behind him was a tall stand of trees. It was a peaceful spot with a light breeze blowing. Just the kind of place a guy could think. His head was buzzing from all the advice he had received over the past few days. Harvey knew the messages were good and the advice well meaning. However, nobody had really told him how to overcome fear or put his head in the water. As a result, he hadn't had a decent meal in days and his stomach was growling. He was having a hard time focusing, let alone knowing what direction to take next, so he sat down and stared at the water.

"Hey you, over there!"

Harvey looked in the direction of the voice and saw a fat raccoon sitting on the edge of a garbage can. "Are you talking to me?" he asked.

"Yeah, you with the long neck and scrawny legs, get over here." The raccoon motioned for Harvey to join him at the garbage can.

Harvey got up, flew to the can,
and landed on the edge opposite the
raccoon.

"Yeah, that's the idea. Now,
reach your head in there
and grab that stuff in
the tinfoil," the raccoon
directed.

Harvey did as
he was told
and handed
the raccoon the
wrapped object.

"Oh, wow!
Corn on the cob,
nice and buttery—my favorite!" The raccoon smacked
his lips and greedily devoured the corn. "What else can
you find down there?"

Harvey reached his head in again and produced a
bone with meat on it.

"Mmm, ribs—my favorite!" The raccoon clapped his
hands and quickly grabbed the ribs from Harvey.

"I thought corn was your favorite," Harvey remarked,
a little annoyed that he was doing all the work and his
stomach was empty.

"Actually, all this leftover picnic food is good. Here, try a piece." The raccoon handed Harvey a tiny piece of meat and then quickly ate the rest.

"It's spicy, but I guess I could get used to it." Harvey was desperate enough to eat anything.

"That's good to know because I have a deal for you. The name's Randy, and I propose we combine our skills and raid all the trash cans around here. We'll split the profits, 70/30." He looked at Harvey, but when Harvey didn't respond, he said, "Okay, so we split 60/40. Think about it. With my brains and your neck, we could own this park."

"It's a good offer. But why do you need a partner? Why don't you just jump in and get it yourself?" Harvey asked.

"Can you keep a secret?" he asked as he looked around. "I'm terrified of falling in. About a year ago, I was really overweight. I reached in a can to get some leftovers and fell in. I was so big that I couldn't climb out. That was on a Sunday night. They didn't pick up the trash until Friday morning. I completely ran out of leftovers and thought I was going to die of starvation. Fortunately, I frightened the garbage collector and he released me. Otherwise, I'd be lunchmeat in some trash compactor."

"Wow, that's harsh. I know about fear. I'm all over it," Harvey sympathized and then admitted his fears about water. "I'd like to help you, but I don't think I'll find any fish in the trash. That's really what I want to eat."

"If it's fish you want, give me a minute to think about it. I've got it!" Randy hit his forehead and pointed toward the water. "Well, duh! Why don't you check out the bucket over there?"

"Seriously! You mean there's fish in that small bucket?" Harvey was shaking with excitement. "How'd they get there?"

"Listen, kid, all the guys that fish in this park keep the ones they don't throw back in a bucket. They're yours for the taking, if you're sly."

"You may have saved my life, Randy. How can I ever thank you?"

"Next time you see me sitting on a trash can, lend me your neck. That's payment enough."

"You've got a deal." Harvey waved to his new friend and excitedly flew to the bucket.

"Hey, kid! Be careful!" Randy jumped from the trash can and yelled again. "I can't watch this. It won't be pretty if you get caught!"

### Randy, the Best Friend:

We may find each other through common interests, shared fears, or a random encounter. If we're lucky, we find someone to share our darkest secrets and revel in our greatest victories. They help us negotiate the twists and turns in life and, hopefully, we do the same for them. Have you found your best friend yet?

Harvey landed a short distance from the bucket. He walked up quietly and peeked inside. There were more fish in that small bucket than he had ever seen at one time. He was so excited he jumped in the air and flapped his wings.

"Food! I'm saved!"

He started to grab a fish when an angry voice came from behind him. He looked up and was startled to see the fisherman waving his arms and running toward the bucket.

"What are you doing, you crazy heron? Get away from my fish! I didn't work all day for you to eat them!"

Harvey wasn't sure what the man was saying, but he

recognized anger and promptly flew away. He didn't go far, just to the edge of the river. He was tired and hungry and didn't have the energy left to fly. He sat down, completely discouraged.

"I'm hopeless, just like everyone said. I'll never make it. I'm so hungry. I should have stayed with Mom and Dad. I wonder if they even miss me?" He was so sad. Harvey completely gave up and cried uncontrollably.

"You poor little heron. You look puny and pathetic," the fisherman said. "I shouldn't have been so mean. I guess most of these fish should have been put back. They're small, but would you like one? Here, catch."

*When we wallow in negativity and self-pity, we lose more than momentum; we lose ourselves.*

From his side vision, Harvey could see something flying at him.

"What's that? Fish?" He jumped up, grabbed it as it flew by, and swallowed it quickly.

"Hey, you catch pretty good. That's kind of cute. Here, try another." The fisherman tossed another fish, and Harvey jumped up and grabbed it. The fisherman laughed as he kept tossing fish to Harvey, who never missed. Finally, the bucket was empty and Harvey was very full.

"Well, that's all I've got. But if you're out here tomorrow, I might see you again."

Harvey didn't know exactly what the guy said, but he was a smart bird. He knew if there was one bucket in the park, there must be more. Now that he had a full stomach and could think clearly, he was determined to find more fish the next day.

The next morning, he got an early start and headed to the same spot. The fisherman was back, and this time he brought friends. Harvey landed in the grass and slowly walked over to them. He hung back, though, because he was afraid they might not accept him. But the fisherman seemed anxious to introduce Harvey to his friends.

"Hey, guys, look! That's the bird I told you about. Watch him catch this fish." The man threw him a small fish he had just pulled off his line. Just as before, Harvey jumped in the air and grabbed it.

"Let me see if he'll take one from me," another man said and tossed Harvey a fish. Harvey moved closer, grabbed the toss, and swallowed.

They all laughed at his antics, and soon Harvey felt comfortable and accepted by the fishermen. All morning he stood around with them, waiting and watching them catch fish. Soon he knew to watch their bobbers. When they bounced, he would jump excitedly to check the size of the fish. They always kept the large ones, but a small one would go to him.

---

### Fishermen, the Parents:

They enable us, but they do so in the most positive sense of the word. No matter how old we get or how mature we think we are, they never stop worrying about us. They praise our achievements, provide a safe haven in a storm, and offer a safety net as we tentatively explore the world. They teach us, nurture us, and help us find the courage to put our heads in the turbulent water of life.

---

As the days passed, Harvey learned about all the fishing areas, and he would fly to each one and check out the catch. He tried to be a friendly heron, and everyone wanted an opportunity to feed him. Boaters and park-goers photographed him, but he loved the fishermen and the time he spent with them. Mostly he loved his full stomach. He would stand on the grass or the rocks by the shore just watching. During slow times, he would sit on the grass and wait for the bobbers to bounce. Everyone fed him, and no one asked him to put his head in the water.

Life was good for Harvey. Even Randy told him he was a lucky bird one morning as he watched Harvey retrieve a cinnamon roll from a trash can.

"I can't believe how good the guys are to me," he said as he handed the food to the raccoon. "I just wish I knew what they were saying. I can understand everyone else, but humans are impossible."

"It's not hard at all," Randy said as he licked the frosting from the roll. "Humans think they're very smart, but they have a limited vocabulary. Usually they're screaming at us to get away. Especially me; they think I carry some weird disease. Like I'd want to bite them and get their germs. When they're not screaming, they use a lot of "in" words. Walkin, talkin, fishin, boatin, eatin, sailin, playin, it just goes on and on. Once you learn the "in" words, the rest is easy. They really have simple minds. You'll learn their language, but they'll never understand yours."

We spend so much energy dodging life's thunderstorms. We should stop for a moment and realize that the rain always brings new growth. If we let the water run off us, the sun will inevitably return and we might just see a rainbow.

Randy was right. Once Harvey paid attention to the speech pattern, he could figure out what they were saying.

One afternoon, he overheard them talking about him. It was the start of autumn and they talked about the days getting shorter and winter arriving soon.

"I wonder what will happen to the heron?" one guy asked.

"I've never seen him catch any fish on his own," another said. "I think he only gets fish when we give them to him."

"I wonder if he'll fly south when we leave for the winter. Then what will he do?"

"He better figure it out, or he'll get pretty cold and hungry. I don't think he'll make it."

Harvey felt panicked for the first time in a long while. He almost wished he didn't know what they were saying.

"What do you mean you're leaving for the winter? What am I supposed to do for food?" he screamed, but they seemed oblivious. He jumped up and down to get their attention.

"Calm down, guy, we'll be catchin' some fish soon," one fisherman said.

"I'm doomed," he thought. "Wait, don't panic. It can't be hopeless. I'll just store up enough fish and maybe hibernate like some of my other friends. I can work this out. I just have to!"

# Chapter Seven

It was a warm Indian summer day in the midst of autumn. The maple leaves were at the height of color, the sky was deep blue, and there was not a hint of breeze. Harvey had spent the morning with a group of friendly guys who were having no luck fishing. By early afternoon, they had left their poles dangling in the water. They were sitting around the picnic table talking and enjoying lunch. No one was paying attention to Harvey, and he was getting very hungry. His hunger was making him irritable. He couldn't understand why they weren't interested in their poles or working harder at fishing. He paced back and forth watching the slow-moving river. Suddenly, a bobber bounced and then another.

"C'mon guys—we've got fish!" Harvey jumped up and down and tried desperately to get their attention. But now they were busy playing cards, talking, and eating sandwiches. They did not seem to care about fishing today.

"Guys, you're letting them get away, and I'm so hungry!" Harvey cried. But nothing he tried, including flapping his wings, got their attention. "Oh, please, come help me!"

It was a defining moment for Harvey.

His stomach was growling, and no matter what he did, he couldn't get their attention. He had to decide in a split second whether to stay safe but hungry or risk it all and conquer his fear. He took a deep breath, closed his eyes, and looked deep inside himself. In that moment he found something that was there all along—courage! He opened his eyes and knew with certainty that he could be brave and strong.

*When our life's hunger outweighs our fears, we find the courage to risk everything and become the person we've wanted to be.*

With a newfound burst of energy, he leaped into the air, flapped his wings, and landed with a thud in the water. He panicked for just a moment, but then he looked down. He didn't sink, nor did he drown. Instead, his long legs touched the bottom of the water and he stood up triumphant with a loud scream of excitement.

"I did it! I'm not afraid!" He quickly grabbed a fish from a line, then another, and still one more all the while avoiding the hooks. Just as quickly, he swallowed the fish. With a big leap, he soared into the air and landed safely on the grass. He shook the water from his wings and gave a satisfied sigh.

"Look at that bird! I've never seen him do that before!" One of the guys left the game as Harvey landed on the grass.

"Wow, he's a smart bird! Imagine that!" another exclaimed.

"We don't have to worry about him after all," yet another joined in.

Harvey beamed at the praise. Meanwhile, Randy jumped up on a nearby trash can and gave him a big thumbs-up.

> When you're paralyzed with fear, ask yourself what's the worst that can happen? If you're like Harvey, you put your head in the water and get your face wet.

"Way to go! If you can do it, I can do it!" he said as he looked back into the trash can. Then, shaking his head, he added, "Nope, not today. I'll deal with the fear thing tomorrow. Today is about you!"

Mother Swan and her almost fully grown children floated by. "Oh, Harvey, you did it!" she exclaimed. "See, children, all it takes is a little confidence in yourself and you can do anything."

stupid, but he sure is strange."

"We're all strange but unique in our own way," Mother Swan scolded. "Just remember, being different is okay."

Gus and Gracie paddled in behind the swans. "Hey, you did it! This calls for a celebration! C'mon!"

Soon the swans and geese had floated around a bend in the river and were piling up on the grass, far away from the fishermen. They were joined by two circling seagulls that wanted to be part of the party. Three turtles crawled up on rocks to sit in the sun alongside them. Randy ran over to a trash can that had a big bag of discarded popcorn hanging from the top. He grabbed the bag and dragged it to the gathering. Soon everyone but Harvey was feasting. As the honored guest, he had to demonstrate his newly acquired skill. Several times, to the cheers of his audience, he dipped his head in the water and caught minnows. In between, he flew back to be with the fishermen. He didn't want them to think he wasn't their friend now that he could fish on his own. They continued to reward him with their attention and several small fish. He couldn't remember when he'd been happier or fuller.

It was his full stomach that caused him to start to walk back toward the others rather than take to the air. As he rounded the bend, he blinked because he couldn't believe what he saw. His past was standing halfway between his present and future.

"Mom and Dad, is that really you?" he screamed with excitement.

"Oh, Harvey, we finally found you!" his mother answered.

"We've looked everywhere for you all summer," his father added.

After an intense round of hugs, Harvey asked, "How did you find me? You must have traveled for miles."

"A couple of young herons thought they saw you fishing with some humans. We had to find out if that was true," Helen replied. "Did you know that the rookery is just over the treetops on the other side of the river?"

"What? You've got to be kidding?" Harvey's eyes widened. "I thought I flew miles away from there."

"We thought you did, too. That's why we went for miles this summer looking for you," Henry admitted.

"Sadly, we failed to realize that when you're young, the most amazing adventures happen in your own backyard."

"The main thing is, you found me. Did you happen to see me fishing?" Harvey asked with obvious pride.

"We flew over just as you put your head in the water. We couldn't believe our eyes," Helen said.

"I guess we know who he gets his remarkable skills from," Henry puffed up his chest.

*Sometimes we travel great lengths to find meaning and direction. If we took a moment to look around, we'd find it's often closer than we think.*

"Must be from the impressive nest builder," Helen whispered to Harvey, who giggled hysterically in response.

"You two aren't laughing at me, are you?" His father lifted an eyebrow.

"No way, Dad. Now, I want you to meet my friends. We'll start with the fishermen."

"Let's not. Humans are scary and evil," Henry said.

"Not these humans. But if you're afraid, we'll start with the others." They headed in the direction of the other group as Harvey caught a flash of white from above. "You go introduce yourselves. I'll be right there."

"Whoa, don't get too close!" B-Cubed warned when Harvey landed next to him in the tree.

"Did you see me put my head in the water?" Harvey landed next to him and started to give him an embrace.

66

"I'll answer if you don't hug me. My talon finally grew back, and I've just survived the most awful molt. My feathers are just starting to regain their former luster," B-Cubed said as he directed Harvey to the other edge of the branch. "But yes, I see you finally got some guts."

"Not only that, I'm ready to challenge you to a fish-off. The winner gets the other guy's fish," Harvey proposed with a crooked smile.

"You're on. Tomorrow at sunrise, same place. Of course, I'll get the most fish. So you'll starve as usual," B-Cubed announced confidently. Then, squinting his eyes, he added, "But I guess you'll cheat and let the humans feed you."

"Maybe," Harvey admitted. "But I do know one thing: I'll see you on the water, old guy!" He laughed loudly as he flew off.

The most wonderful day of his life was ending too quickly. The sun was dipping low in the sky and promising a spectacular fall sunset as the groups started to break up. The fishermen had packed up and waved goodbye to Harvey, telling him they'd see him the next day. Mother Swan had insisted her almost-adult youngsters follow her to a secluded spot to get some early sleep. Randy said he smelled the embers of an old campfire and that there was a leftover hot dog with his name on it. Before he ran off, he said farewell to everyone and promised he'd get Harvey's secret to overcoming fear the next day. Gus and Gracie joined a flock of honking geese and were soon flying in a beautiful V formation across the cloudless orange and purple streaked sky. Offshore, the seagulls were floating in the water, awaiting nightfall and the beginning of their cleanup duties.

Only Harvey and his parents remained. They stood together watching the setting sun, reluctant to let the amazing day end. To break the stillness, Harvey posed a question his friend Spike had asked of him.

"Mom, Dad, what do you see when you look in front of you?"

His father answered first. "It's a gorgeous sunset. I don't remember ever seeing that many colors before. It seems the days are getting shorter, and I feel a bit more chill in the air. Before long the water will be frozen and we'll need to fly south. I think this first year, you should follow us, Son."

"Henry, maybe we should follow him. I think he gets his adventurous spirit from my side," Helen interrupted. Then, turning to Harvey, she added, "You asked the question, dear. So, what do you see?"

"I see my family. We're not perfect, but we love each

other, and I'm glad to have you back. And I have more friends than I ever imagined. We're all very different, and I know we'll separate for a while. But we'll be back together in the spring because we've found a place where the food is plentiful. Everyone here is helpful and nobody is hopeless, especially me. I've found my rainbow. I've explored all the beautiful layers and followed the twists and turns. Better still, I see the end of the rainbow. And I've found the very best place to be."


Perception
is the largest part
of our reality.
Every person's vision
is special and individual.
What do you see when
you look in front of you?
Have you found
your rainbow yet?

# Author Note

The inspiration for this book is loosely based on the lives of two unique characters. The first is Harvey, a blue heron, that spends his summers at Kensington Metropark in Milford, Michigan. With his fearless in-your-face attitude, he has provided countless hours of enjoyment for fishermen, boaters, and parkgoers. In the process, he has ensured a good life and a steady supply of his own brand of "happy meals."

The second is Spike, a lop-eared rabbit, who escaped a sad existence by taking an enormous risk. He followed my black cat home one summer morning and found the home of his dreams, a buffet of his favorite munchies, and a warm afternoon snuggle with his best, though potentially dangerous, friend.

These two remarkable beings have led me to believe that all creatures on this planet hunger for more than a good meal. We want to find our purpose in life and have a chance to shape our own unique destinies. Doing so is never without risk and sacrifice, but it's what makes the accomplishment that much sweeter. So in closing, I wish for you what I hope for myself. Be adventurous and go face first toward that vision you see in front of you. Embrace the journey and all the twists and turns along the way. Always remember that finding the end of your rainbow is all about how you handle the curve.

# About the Author

Michele Olzack is a native of Michigan who received her BSN and MS from the University of Michigan. After a lengthy career as a Nurse Practitioner in Women's Health and Urology, she finds her greatest joy is the leisure time she spends outdoors. Whether it's gardening, sailing, kayaking, biking, or skiing, she finds the inspiration for her writing, photography, and painting in the natural world. With this first book, she's spreading her wings and putting her head in the water, and she sincerely hopes that the worst that happens is she gets a very wet face.

For more information about Michele, please visit,
www.micheleolzackbooks.com